It's All So Bittersweet

Ian Rose Castro

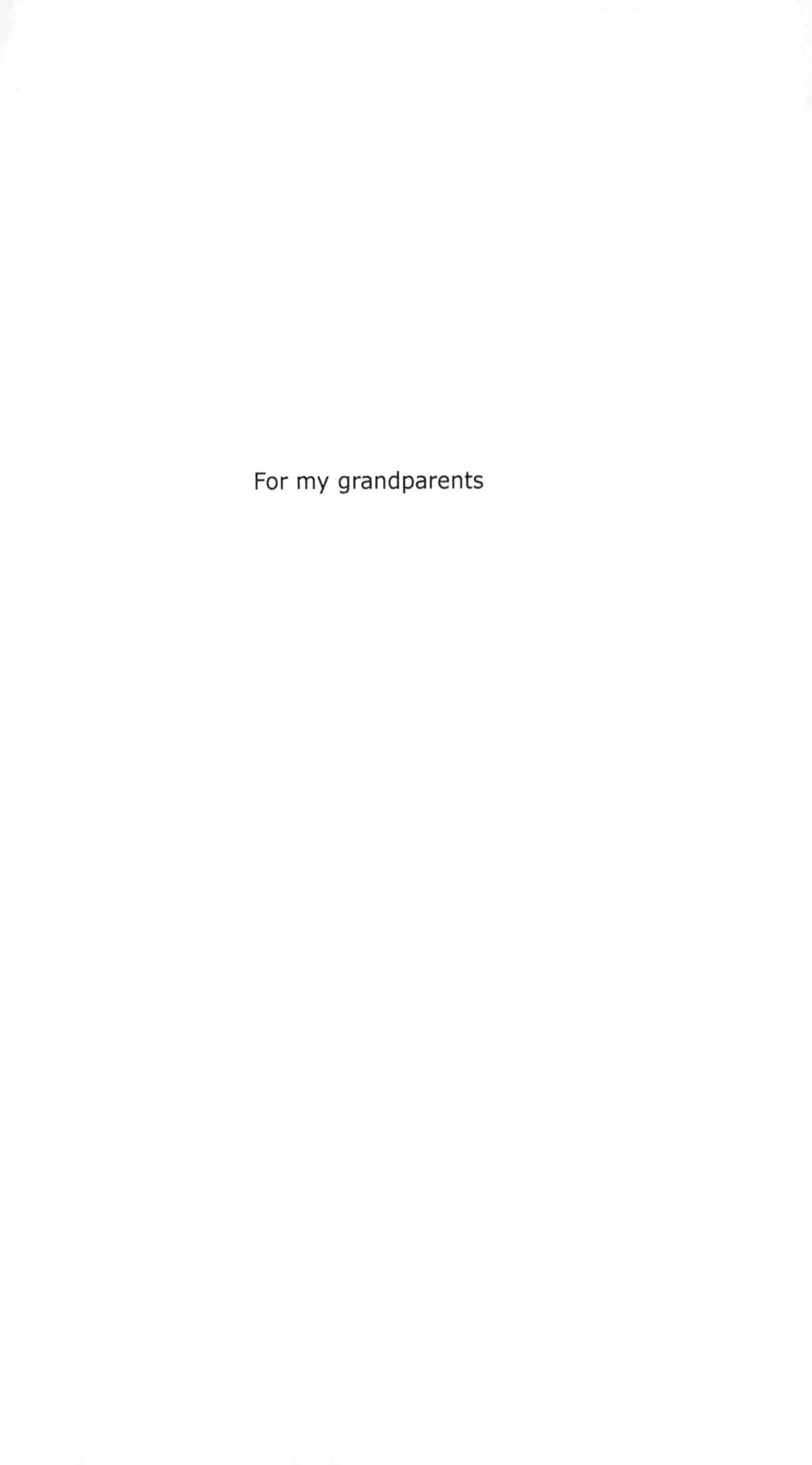

For my grandparents

Previous Woodview Stories

Book One

It Could Always Be Worse

After a traumatic experience in her home town of Miami, Elena Flores moves away to live with the father she's never met. It's not easy starting a new school in the middle of October, so when her half-sister invites her to a party, she thinks "what's the worst that could happen?"

Book Two

Will It Ever Get Better?

Jo Reilly has dealt with a lot of big changes lately. She's sharing a room with a surprise half-sister, her parents are always fighting, her best friends aren't speaking to her, and she's falling for someone totally unexpected. All she wants is to be normal, but what does that even mean?

It's All So Bittersweet

A Woodview Story

by Ian Rose Castro

Playlist

Track 1: It's My Party by Lesley Gore

Track 2: Introvert Party Club by RODAN

Track 3: Paradise by Coldplay

Track 4: All Good Things (Come To An End) by Nelly Furtado

Track 5: Speak Now by Taylor Swift

Track 6: Under Pressure by David Bowie and Queen

Track 7: Perfect by Simple Plan

Track 8: Go Your Own Way by Fleetwood Mac

Track 9: Ordinary World by Duran Duran

Track 10: Unavoidable by Neon Trees

Track 11: Play Pretend by Alex Sampson

Track 12: Secrets by Mary Lambert

Track 13: Stressed Out by Twenty One Pilots

Track 14: Hanging By A Moment by Lifehouse

Track 15: Last Dance by Donna Summer

Part One:

Before

1

It's My Party

Jo

This is a disaster. My dress is way too big. It's terrible! Okay, it's not *terrible*, but it's not good either. It isn't hanging on me the way it should be, especially considering that I got it tailored to my exact size. Or I guess, to the exact size I *used* to be? How did this even happen? I was so worried that I might gain too much weight, that I hadn't even considered losing too much weight could be a possibility.

Any other day I'd be kind of happy to realize I lost a few pounds. I'd be thrilled, really. But today? Today it's horrible, awful news. Today is my sweet sixteen. It's supposed to be an absolutely perfect day, but the party hasn't even started yet and everything is already going all wrong.

"No one's even gonna notice," Elena lies, attempting to calm me down. "If it's bothering you that much, I can add a few stitches to tighten the bust a bit, but I really don't think it's necessary."

Elena does not appreciate how important a girl's sweet sixteen is, not even after my parents decided that this party would be honoring her as well. I understand why they did that. When we first started planning it, they didn't know they would have a second daughter turning sixteen in the same year. It was too late (and probably too expensive) to pull together a second event only a few months later. She probably wouldn't have even wanted her own party anyway. She definitely doesn't want to be involved in this one, but my mom insisted that she be included. So my sweet sixteen became our sweet sixteen.

I'd be lying if I said sharing this with her didn't bother me a little bit. It bothers me a lot. It's not like we're twins. It's *my* birthday. Her birthday isn't for another *two months*. Why should we have to celebrate together?

"Do you think you could?" I ask. "I don't want it to look like we had to have it altered."

"You already did have it altered, by the tailor," she points out. I hate when she uses logic against me.

"Yes, but he was a professional. Do you even know how to sew?"

"Would I have offered to fix your dress if I didn't know how to sew?" She laughs.

I don't see how this is funny, but I force myself to halfheartedly join in anyway. I guess it wouldn't hurt to lighten up a little bit. One issue is not going to ruin the entire day. Or at least that's what I'm going to keep telling myself. If I say it enough times, maybe I'll start to believe it. I really want it to be true.

"I'm just going to do a tiny alteration, just a few stitches." Elena walks over to me and pulls at the side of my dress until it is perfectly snug. "No one will even see it."

I sigh. "You better be right."

Just then, there's a knock at the door and before either of us can even say "come in," it opens. I spin around as my mom walks in with my cousin Kate in tow. Kate excitedly runs to me, wrapping me in a big hug and almost knocking Elena over in the process.

"Happy birthday!" she squeals. Technically, it's not actually my birthday for two more weeks and Kate knows that, but she'll be back in Chicago before then, so we'll both pretend that it's really today. "You look amazing!"

Elena poorly suppresses a chuckle and I know exactly what she's thinking. Maybe now that Kate has said it, I'll actually believe it. And she's a little bit right. Kate telling me I look good holds a lot more weight than Elena telling me does, because Kate and I are much more similar than Elena and I are. Elena doesn't care about appearances the way I do, because, unlike me, she's effortlessly pretty.

Her long, wavy, dark brown hair always does what she wants it to. It even looks perfect when she's just woken up. Meanwhile my blonde hair always falls flat and limp. She's curvy, but in the right places, unlike me. Being half Puerto Rican, it's like she has a year round tan, while I'm pale and always burn in the sun. And although she doesn't usually wear a lot of makeup (because she doesn't need to), today my mom insisted that she get her hair and makeup done, so now she looks even more beautiful than usual, which is so unfair.

On the other hand, Kate is just like me. We have the same blonde hair, same pale skin. We look a lot more like sisters than Elena and I do. So if Kate thinks I look great, then maybe I actually do look somewhat okay.

"Thank you," I smile. I'm still going to have Elena fix it, but I don't tell Kate that.

"Is Marisol here yet?" Kate asks. "I'm so excited to meet her!"

"Them," I correct. "Marisol is nonbinary, remember?"

"Okay, whatever, sorry." Kate says, just slightly rolling her eyes. "Are they here or not?"

"No, but they'll be here later for the party. You can meet them then."

Kate looks confused. "Shouldn't they be here early to prepare for the entrance? Aren't they going to escort you?"

I shake my head. "Actually my friend Nico's gonna do that," I explain. "You remember Nico, right?"

She nods slowly.

I asked Nico to be my escort a long time ago, before he even started dating my friend Rachel. We aren't as close as we used to be, but he's still one of my oldest friends and my only long-term guy friend. Our mothers have been best friends since they were in high school, so we've practically known each other since birth. It just made sense to ask him. At least, it made sense at the time.

Once I started dating Marisol, I considered asking them to take Nico's place and do it instead. I know Nico wouldn't have minded, but my dad didn't think it was a good idea. He said he didn't want to cause any drama with my grandparents on my "special night," but I think he just doesn't want to admit that Marisol makes him uncomfortable. Or not Marisol specifically, so much as the idea of me dating anyone who isn't a guy. After some convincing, my mom decided that he had a good point about keeping the night drama-free. Once they outnumbered me, I didn't have a chance. My parents haven't agreed on much lately, but somehow they managed to agree on that.

Aside from Kate, I haven't told any of my extended family that I'm a lesbian. Dad thought it was best to wait. The news will probably go over a lot better if I don't do a surprise reveal during my sweet sixteen entrance. Although I think he secretly wishes I'll wait forever.

Kate shrugs. "I just assumed you'd be telling people by now."

"Oh, uh… no, not yet." I smile and force a slight laugh, trying to act like this is no big deal, but suddenly I feel uncomfortable.

"Your dad's here too, by the way," my mom interjects, taking advantage of the sudden lull in conversation. I'd forgotten she was even here. "I just thought you both should know, in case you want to go downstairs to see him." She smiles weakly and it's clear that she's not really thinking about me right now.

It's been months since Elena showed up on our doorstep in tears asking if she could stay the night. Ever since then, she's been living with us, instead of at our dad's apartment like she's supposed to be. I guess whatever happened between them must've been really serious, but she hasn't wanted to talk about it.

Whatever their problem is, they better not let it ruin the party.

2

Introvert Party Club

Elena

Today really should have just been about Jo. I already take up so many of her spaces. We share a bedroom, a school... She shouldn't need to lose half of her sweet sixteen to me as well.

It's not like this party has anything to do with me anyway. It's just the title. Anyone can tell that Jo obviously chose everything.

She said pink is her signature color, so she is wearing a pink dress. She decided that I would wear silver, so we'd match the pink and silver decorations, which, of course, she also chose. She even chose the signature cocktails. Yes, that's cocktails, plural. This sweet sixteen has three signature cocktails (and of course, mocktails, because the majority of the guests aren't even old enough to drink alcohol). There's the Sweet Sixteeni, the Jojito, and the Ellini which are basically just a watermelon martini, a strawberry mojito, and a raspberry bellini. All three are pink, including the one named after me, because Jo even chose *my* signature cocktail. And I let her, because I don't care what drinks are served at this party because it's *her* party. It's ridiculous that we're pretending it's anything other than that.

The only thing I tried to give a little bit of input on was the music. I don't care if the whole room looks like someone vomited pink and silver glitter all over it (and it does). I don't care if my dress is ridiculous (and it is). But I do care about the music. If I have to be at this party, there might as well be a few songs playing that I like. She accepted about a third of my suggestions, which is way more than I expected, to be honest. I don't have a problem taking a backseat to Jo on all this. It's her big day. It's like this is Jo's wedding and I'm her least favorite bridesmaid.

I tried to explain that I didn't need a sweet sixteen, and I certainly didn't need to co-opt Jo's, but Meg wouldn't take no for an answer. She always does her best to treat me the same way she treats Jo, as if I am her actual daughter who has always been part of her family, instead of the surprise stepdaughter that she met less than a year ago.

I appreciate it. Really, I do. But sometimes I wish there was less for me to appreciate. I don't deserve to be treated this well after I upended her life. She's not my mom. She's not even really my stepmom anymore because she and my dad are separated. She shouldn't have to do all this for me.

Looking back, I wish I hadn't gone to their house the night my dad and I had our big fight. I said I didn't know where else to go, which felt true at the time, but in hindsight, there were plenty of other places I could have gone. Ren and his dad definitely would have let me stay over. I probably could've gone to any of my friends' houses. Even Levi would have let me in, although that might have felt too weird. The last (and first, and only) time I slept at his house was the night that he stopped Dylan from doing the unthinkable while I was passed out drunk. He helped me then, I know he would've helped me again. Although his help probably would have made me feel as guilty as Meg's help does. My friendship with Levi is weird. I'm not sure if it could ever feel completely normal.

But I didn't go to him or any of my other friends. I went to Meg. Now she is stuck taking care of me because my dad won't.

"Are you excited?" Ren asks, snapping me back to reality.

"I guess so."

As we stand in the back room waiting for the grand entrance, all I can think is that I shouldn't even be here.

"Come on Elena, you know this is pretty cool." I think Ren is just excited to be at a sweet sixteen. He didn't have a lot of friends before I moved here and the friends he did have won't be turning sixteen for another year. "Although I guess you'd probably rather be here with someone else." He looks down at his shoes.

"You're my best friend," I reassure him. "There's no one I'd rather be here with. I just don't really want to be here at all."

He gives his signature sad smile. The one he gives when he's trying to make everyone think he's happy, instead of upset about something he'll never ever talk about. I don't know what's making him upset today, but even if I ask, he won't tell me.

I think that's what makes our friendship work. We can tell each other anything, but we don't. Or at least we don't have to. He hasn't pressured me to talk about the fight I had with my dad and I haven't pressured him to talk about... whatever it is that he's avoiding talking about.

"I'm so happy you're here," I say as I give his hand a little squeeze.

He smiles. "Me too."

3

Paradise

Jo

I can hear our guests filling the banquet hall and suddenly I feel like I can barely breathe. I glance over at Elena. She looks perfectly calm, talking and laughing with Ren. I wish I could be more like her. She's going to have a great time at this party — *my* party — and I'll probably be too stressed out to enjoy it.

Sometimes I wonder if Elena is afraid of anything. She never seems to get nervous, even in extreme situations, which we both know she's been through her fair share of. She would never panic about a silly party.

I feel a hand on my shoulder and look over at Nico. "You okay?"

I nod, but he doesn't buy it for a second. We've known each other long enough that he can tell when I'm completely full of shit.

"What's wrong?" he continues. "Tonight's gonna be awesome. You know that, right?"

"Yeah," I say, "I guess." I take a seat on a nearby bench and look down at the floor, so he won't see that I'm still lying.

He sits down next to me. "You don't have to be so nervous."

"I'm not nervous."

"Sure you're not," he says sarcastically.

At first I think he's mocking me, but when I glance back at him I see that he's looking at me with genuine concern, like he actually cares about whatever it is I'm going through right now.

Nico and I aren't particularly close. In fact, we aren't close at all. Not anymore. The only reason we ever hung out as kids was because our moms were best friends. Now when I see him it's usually just because he's my friend's boyfriend, not because he's my friend. Even when I asked him to be my escort, it was really more like my mom asked his mom, and she probably guilt-tripped him into saying yes. I highly doubt he would have agreed if he had a choice. I think he just considers me an acquaintance he's forced to be around sometimes.

I sigh. "It just feels like today isn't going the way it's supposed to."

"What do you mean?"

I shrug, although I know exactly what I mean. When my family and I started planning this party, everything was so different. My parents weren't separated. Casey was still my best friend. I didn't know I had a half-sister. No one knew I was a lesbian, not even me really. I mean, I guess I always knew, but I wasn't ready to admit it to myself, let alone anyone else.

When we first started planning this party, life still felt easy.

"Is this about Marisol?" he asks. "I know you'd probably rather have her, sorry, *them* here instead of me."

I shake my head. "That wouldn't have been a good idea."

"Why not? I thought your parents were cool with it and everything."

"They are," I assure him. "It's just that the rest of my family doesn't know yet and my dad thinks I should wait a little bit longer to tell them. I mean, his parents are very traditional. I'm not sure what they'd say. It could ruin the whole night."

"Oh." His demeanor changes suddenly. He somehow looks smaller. "I didn't realize you still had problems like that. I'm sorry."

"It's fine. Marisol probably wouldn't have wanted to do it anyway."

That gets Nico to smile. "Yeah, they don't exactly seem like the type to be into this kind of thing. You guys are pretty... different."

Before I have a chance to really think about what he just said, someone comes around to inform us that it is time to line up for our entrances. Nico stands and extends his hand to me like I'm a princess getting out of a carriage to go to a ball. It feels like an odd allusion of an alternate universe where my life went the way I thought it would. As a little kid, when I pictured my sweet sixteen, I figured I'd have a boyfriend and some amazing lifelong friends and a happy family, but that just wasn't in the cards for me. I guess not everything can go according to plan.

4

All Good Things Come To An End

Ren

I might not be good at many things, but I like to think of myself as someone who is good with words. But there are no words I could use to fully describe just how much Elena Mariana Flores does not want to be here tonight.

One would have to be completely lacking in observational skills and situational awareness to not notice that Elena is miserable. If she could will the floor to crack open and swallow her up whole, she would. I have to keep reminding myself that she is unhappy, not because she doesn't want to be here *with me*, but rather because she just doesn't want to be here at all. Although, if I'm being honest, she probably wouldn't mind being here with someone else. I don't say that to be down on myself, even though I usually am pretty down on myself. I say that because I know she couldn't exactly ask her secret boyfriend to be her escort, even if he's not actually very secret at all. I think the only people who still think their relationship is a secret... are them.

"Try to enjoy it," I tell her, knowing that nothing I say right now will have any effect on her mood in any way whatsoever.

It's times like these that I wonder if I'm not a good enough friend to her. A good friend would be able to make her feel better, but I can't do that. I'm useless when it comes to things like that. It is one of the many things I am not good at.

Maybe I'm just out of practice at being a good friend because I haven't had anyone to be a good friend to in so long. Elena is the first real friend I've had since I was in seventh grade.

I glance over at Nico without realizing I'm doing it. Luckily he's too busy talking to Jo to notice me. Maybe I was naïve for thinking that Nico and I would always be friends. I'm not that naive anymore. It would be nice to believe that Elena and I could be friends forever, but eventually I'll do something to ruin it, just like I ruined everything with Nico. It's hard to believe I haven't ruined it already.

I thought for sure that I had, when I kissed her a few months ago. I don't even like her like that... Why do I do such foolish things? Through some incredible stroke of luck I didn't scare her off and we are still friends. Now I am determined to be as great of a friend as possible, for as long as possible. I never want her to start hating me the way Nico does.

"Earth to Ren." Elena snaps me out of my dramatic internal monologue. "We have to line up now."

"Oh, right." I get up and stand behind Jo and Nico. I wonder if there was any discussion about who would enter first. Jo probably didn't give Elena a say in the matter, but Elena doesn't seem to care that she's second because Elena doesn't seem to care about any of this.

"Are you ready?" I ask, putting on a smile.

"No," she replies instantly, but then a sense of realization hits her face and she tries to cover. "I mean, yeah. I'm ready. Let's do this!"

I would find her crazy overcorrection kind of comical, if I didn't know that she is putting on this facade to hide how sad she really is. I want to ask her about it, but I'm always afraid of pushing her away. She has a tendency to run and hide when she feels cornered. Sometimes metaphorically, sometimes literally.

"I can tell that you're kind of stressed." I try to choose my words carefully, but nothing ever comes out of my mouth as eloquently as it is in my head. "Are you just stressed about the party or are you stressed... about..." I hesitate, not sure how I should end this question, "...something else?"

"It's just the party," she lies, looking down at the floor.

Obviously, I know she's lying. And she knows that I know she's lying. But I don't know if she wants me to pretend I don't know she's lying or if she wants me to press her to tell the truth.

She hasn't spoken to me at all about her dad and the fight they had, even though it occurred months ago. I feel like I should continue to try to find out what happened, but I already tried that, with no success. Eventually, I stopped trying. I don't want to push her to talk about it before she's ready. At least that's the main reason I haven't pried deeper. There's also a second reason, a more selfish reason. I'm afraid if I push her to talk about her dad, she will in turn, push me to talk about my disastrous family life.

So instead I pretend that I don't know she's lying. Does that make me a bad friend? I want to be a good friend, but I'm not sure I even know how.

Part Two:

During

5

Speak Now

Marisol

Sweet sixteens are actually kind of stupid if you think about it. Why should this birthday be any more special than any other birthday? It's not even a round number. And why is it called a *sweet* sixteen? There's nothing that sweet about being sixteen. Sixteen is a terrible age. You still can't drink alcohol or smoke cigarettes or buy a lottery ticket or vote. In some places you can get your driver's license, but not here. So that really doesn't seem like a good enough reason to throw a giant party like this. It's excessive.

I know that tonight is important to Jo so I'm trying to play the role of supportive partner, but I just don't understand her at all sometimes.

I impatiently tap my fingers on the table I'm seated at with the rest of our friends, as we wait for Jo and Elena to make their grand entrance. What kind of a party needs a grand entrance anyway? It's as if they're being announced to society as part of some twisted debutante ball. Of course, they're both being escorted by guys in some bullshit display of heteronormative tradition. Elena is being escorted by Ren Hayashi, who she isn't even dating. One, because he's gay. Two, because we all know who Elena actually likes. Or at least I know. She's not as good at keeping a secret as she thinks she is.

Jo is being escorted by Nico Roma, a guy who isn't even that nice to her and is dating someone else. And Jo is also dating someone else. Me! Fifty percent of the people up there are gay, but they're walking down the aisle together like they're about to get married. It's actually kind of gross when you think about it.

"Are you okay?" Ollie asks. I guess I must be making a face if even he can see right through me.

"Of course I am," I lie. "Isn't this great?" I don't know if he is actually convinced or just humoring me, but either way, he shrugs his giant shoulders and smiles, turning back to his plate which is piled high with tiny hot dogs and mini quiches.

No one could really blame me for being irritated by all of this, right? These kinds of parties are ridiculous. It's not my scene at all. Everything is pink and sparkly, even Jo herself.

I watch her and Nico walk through the banquet hall holding hands. She gives me a little wave as she passes our table and I wave back, putting on a fake smile.

Jo is dressed in a light pink, glittery, poofy dress like a pretty pretty princess. Her normally straight blonde hair has been curled into golden ringlets around her shoulders and she's wearing a bit too much makeup, which I guess you're supposed to do at an event like this.

She looks beautiful of course. She always looks beautiful. But I can't help but think that she's completely overdone it. This is a birthday party, not a coronation. Who does she think she is? I can't believe I am actually dating someone who would be into something like this.

Elena is wearing a very similar dress, which I'm sure was Jo's doing. I can't imagine she'd pick out anything like that herself. I doubt Elena wanted to match the decorations.

She looks like she doesn't really want to be here either. It *is* kind of weird. For one, her actual birthday isn't for months. And it's got to be awkward sharing a sweet sixteen with someone you didn't even know existed a year ago. Plus, Elena hates to be the center of attention and things have been weird with her family since... well, since she learned they were her family in the first place. But they've been extra weird the last few months. She hasn't told us much about what is going on, but it clearly isn't good.

Honestly, I'm surprised they're even having a sweet sixteen, considering all the drama they've been through together. But then again, I can't understand why anyone would want to have a sweet sixteen in the first place. *I* didn't have one. Zeke didn't have one. Ollie didn't have one. Even Violet isn't having one and her mom did everything she possibly could to convince her. Her mom is a lot like Jo in that way. She loves all this girly shit, but Violet doesn't. She's more like me in that way.

Jo and Elena finish making their rounds and join us at the table.

"Hey birthday girls," Zeke says in a sing-song voice. "Time to dance!" He grabs Elena's hand with one hand and Jo's with the other and pulls them both toward the dance floor. I reluctantly follow. I don't want to ruin the night for everyone else, but it's really hard for me to pretend that this whole thing isn't idiotic.

"You look beautiful," I tell Jo. She blushes. I notice she's wearing the gold heart-shaped locket I gave her for Christmas, even though it doesn't quite match the pink and silver theme.

Now I feel kind of guilty. She deserves to feel special tonight.

"What did you think of the entrance?" Jo asks in a small but hopeful voice.

"Oh it was great! Everything was perfect. What an awesome party."

I hope I sound convincing.

6

Under Pressure

Kevin

When Joanne told me that she was a lesbian, I didn't know how to react. I have nothing against gay people. I just never imagined that my daughter was one of them. I'm trying my best to be supportive, but I'm not sure I know how. My parents are very traditional and they raised me to be that way too. I don't want Joanne to be unnecessarily embarrassed in front of everyone, especially not on a day like today.

They're still recovering from the news that I have an illegitimate daughter from a past relationship. I love Elena of course, but my family doesn't believe in premarital sex and they *really* don't believe that children should be born out of wedlock. That's why Meg and I got married when we learned she was pregnant with Joanne. Because I'd always been told that that's what you're supposed to do. I didn't know that Maria was already pregnant with Elena. I couldn't have ever predicted that would happen.

But now she's here and my private business is public. Elena and I can't escape the prying and judgmental eyes of the Reillys, but Joanne still has a chance to keep her private business *private*. I don't want her to throw away that option on a whim.

That's why I told her not to ask her girlfriend to be her escort. Not because I don't approve of the relationship, but because I know my parents wouldn't. What would they say? What would everyone think? I just didn't want her to cause a scene.

This night is supposed to be all about Joanne– I mean Joanne and Elena. I didn't want the party to be ruined by my mother and father saying something that offends her. They're not bad people. They're just old fashioned. They're traditional. They're set in their ways. They're not going to understand something like two girls dating. They're certainly not going to understand the whole non-binary thing. I still don't even understand it. Keeping it all a secret is the best way to protect Joanne.

"What a lovely entrance," my mother leans in and says to me. "Joanne looks beautiful."

"For the price of those dresses, they better look great." I chuckle.

"Of course Elena looks good." She gestures towards her own dress. "Some of us need to pick our clothing more carefully to go with our skin tones. But you know those people look good in any color."

I flinch as she calls Elena *those people*. This is her granddaughter she's talking about.

"You look great, mom."

"Is Joanne dating that handsome young man?"

"I don't think so, mom."

"Oh well, it's probably for the best. He doesn't look Irish. Probably Italian."

"Yes, he's Italian, mom. You've met him a few times. That's Sal and Angela's son," I remind her. "You remember Angela, Meg's best friend from high school."

"Oh, I can't be expected to keep track of everyone you and that Meg knew in high school."

"You've met her dozens of times. She was the maid of honor at our wedding."

"But that was such a rushed wedding. Who could even remember anything?" She crosses her arms. "And look how it all turned out."

I need a break from her, so I get up and head over to the bar.

"Scotch, rocks."

"I'm so sorry sir, we don't actually have any scotch tonight," says the bartender, who barely looks older than Joanne and Elena.

"Do you have *any* kind of whiskey?"

"No, unfortunately we don't. Would you like to try the Jojito? Or the Ellini?"

I sigh. "Vodka tonic?"

"Coming right up, sir."

This is going to be a long night.

7

Perfect

Elena

I think I might actually be having a good time. I basically haven't left the dance floor since the grand entrance. It's a great way to avoid thinking about your problems. I highly recommend it. The only downside is that I'm starting to feel absolutely exhausted. But if I leave the safety zone where I'm surrounded by my friends, I'll have to deal with Meg trying to force me into a conversation with my dad. Or worse, I'll have to talk to any member of his extended family. It's definitely a lot better to stay here, listening to a pop song I sort of know and watching my friends jump around like idiots. But eventually the music shifts to something softer and the deejay announces that it's time to line up for the buffet, so everyone begins to exit the dance floor. I guess that means I also have to.

I stick close to my friends, using them as some kind of human shield. None of them quite know why I'm avoiding my dad, but they know enough to be down to help me do it, no questions asked.

"Are you having fun?" Ollie smiles a big, goofy grin as he shovels pasta onto his plate.

I smile, genuinely. "Yeah. Yeah, I think I am."

"You *think*?" Ren teases.

I nudge him with my elbow. "Shut up. I'm having fun. I am."

"Good," Brooke says, putting her arm around me and pulling me into a hug. I'm glad she and I have become such great friends finally, considering how rocky our relationship used to be. She's a really good person to be around; always there to comfort everyone, make us laugh, cheer us up. Her friendship is one I'd really like to keep.

I realize how truly lucky I am to have each of these people in my life. I didn't think I would find a group of friends as great as my one back home in Miami, but I did. Meg had suggested I invite some of my old friends to come to the party, but I didn't want anyone to feel pressured to spend the money on a flight to New York. Maybe I can visit them this summer instead. I also didn't want them to see how toxic things are with my dad. At least my friends here pretend not to notice, even if I know they do. I would not have gotten through the past few months without them.

I look down at my plate that I've loaded up with a bunch of different foods that Jo picked out. I miss my mother's cooking. The lights begin to dim and I realize that the slideshow Meg has prepared is starting. She'd asked me for photos from my childhood a while ago and I'd given her some, but I still expected it to mainly focus on Jo. I should've known that with Meg in charge that wouldn't be the case.

It opens with side-by-side baby pictures of each of us, which fade into a photo of us together from this past Christmas Eve. Various transition effects take us through dozens of more photos from over the years. Most of the pictures of me were taken since I've moved here (which makes sense because I didn't really give Meg much to work with), but there are also some of me with my Miami friends and some of me as a little kid. I notice that there are even more than just the ones I gave her. I think she must have reached out to my friends for help. There are a few photos of me with my mom, which makes me tear up a little bit. I wish she was here. Or really, I wish neither of us were here and we were both somewhere else entirely, together.

There are a lot more childhood photos of Jo, from holiday gatherings, dance recitals, family vacations... I feel a lump forming in my throat when yet another photo of young Jo smiling in our dad's arms appears on screen. It seems like he was a really good dad to her.

Growing up, I never really cared that I didn't have a father. My mom was amazing, so why would I have ever needed anything more? But sitting here watching a montage of Jo growing up with our dad and me growing up without one, I think about how unfair this all is. I deserved to have that. I deserved a dad who came to all of my piano recitals and took me trick-or-treating and brought me on family vacations. I deserved all of that. And now that I'm here, now that there is finally a chance for me to have that, he still won't be the dad I deserve.

The song playing in the video is fairly quiet, so it draws the attention of everyone on our side of the banquet hall when I abruptly slide my chair out and stand up, but I don't even care. I run out of the room as fast as I can. I just need to be anywhere else but here.

I don't realize that I'm being followed until the door doesn't slam behind me. I turn around to find that all of my friends have run out to the lobby as well, even Jo. They all came after me.

Jo pushes her way to the front of the group and wraps me in a tight hug.

"I'm sorry," I say. "This is stupid. Go back inside. I don't want to ruin your party."

"*Our* party," Jo corrects me. "I'm not going back in until I know you're okay." I stare at her, incredulously. There's no way she's willing to miss her party for me.

"I'm fine."

"You're obviously not fine," Ren says, coming closer to me.

"Is this about your mom?" Brooke asks.

"It's not about her," I whisper.

"Then what is it?" she asks.

Zeke walks forward and holds my hand. I look up into his eyes, and then back at everyone else. They're all standing there worried about me. They left the party just to make sure I was okay. And they actually care. So why have I been keeping this all bottled up inside?

"A few months ago my dad and I got into this really big fight," I say. "The whole time I've lived here, I've felt like there was this wall between us. I thought it was all in my head, but one night I just snapped. I asked him why he keeps pushing me away." The tears start falling uncontrollably. "We argued for a while.

He claimed that wasn't what he was doing, but I insisted that it was. I said it didn't feel like he even wanted to be my dad." My voice breaks, as the story becomes nearly impossible to continue. "And then he finally admitted it. He doesn't. He doesn't want to be my dad at all."

Jo looks like she's about to cry too. "Elena, that can't be true."

"It is," I insist. "He said it. He tried to take it back afterwards, but he said it."

I remember the night perfectly. His words are burned into my mind. So is the way his face looked when he said it. It might've been the first truly honest thing I'd ever heard him say.

"There's too much pain here!" he'd shouted. "Everytime I look at you all I feel is pain. It's torture! How can you expect me to pretend like nothing is wrong and I'm happy you're here? Of course I'm not happy you're here!"

His words hung in the air, but his face softened immediately. I saw the regret in his eyes. "Elena, that came out wrong," he said. "I didn't mean it like that."

But he did. I know he did. Now the truth is out there and it can't be unsaid. I can't even blame him for how he feels. At least there's no point hoping for him to ever be the dad I need anymore. I know he won't. He doesn't even want to.

8

Go Your Own Way

Meg

I glare at Kevin, anger seething through me. I storm across the room and grab onto his arm. "Outside. Now."

He gives me an odd look. "What's going on?"

"We need to talk," I insist. "Come with me."

He doesn't move, so I take matters into my own hands and pull his arm until he's forced to follow me out.

"Jesus, what's gotten into you?"

"You have to get it together. Now."

He sighs. "I'm doing my best here, Meg. Same as you."

I shake my head. "No you're not," I scoff. "I don't think you're trying at all anymore. Do you know what Jo just told me? Elena was just out here crying!"

"She was?" he asks. "What happened?"

"You happened!" I shout. "You hurt her, Kevin. Can't you see that? The things you said to her, they're eating her up inside. But you wouldn't know that because you haven't been there!" I turn away. I can't even stand to look at him anymore.

"Hey!" He puts his hand on my shoulder and forces me to turn around to face him again. "We both agreed that her staying with you and Joanne was what was best for her."

"I thought you meant for a few days, just to give you some space away from each other so you could both cool off," I explain. "But

Kevin, it's been months. She needs her father back."

He sits down on a bench near the wall and drops his head. He's quiet for a long time, but I won't back down. I just stand there, staring at him, until he dares to speak again.

"I don't know how to be her dad." His voice is so quiet I can barely hear it.

"Well figure it out."

He looks up at me, clapping his hands together. "Why? She doesn't need me. She's better off without me."

I sit down next to him. "Why would you think that?"

He closes his eyes. "I'm not her father," he says. "Not really. Not in any way that matters."

"Don't do that. Don't do that self pitying bullshit."

"It's true," he insists. "I was never there for her. How am I supposed to just pick up and start now? All I can think about when I'm with her is all the things I did wrong... all the things I missed."

"If you're so worried about that, why do you continue to do the wrong things and miss even more?"

"That's not fair."

"You can't change the past, Kevin." I place my hand on his knee. "But you can try to make up for it. And you've got to start somewhere."

He takes a deep breath and turns his head away from me. "It's just so hard." He turns back to look at me again and I see that there are tears in his eyes. "It's so hard to look at her when all I see is Maria looking back at me."

"I know it's hard for you," I admit, "but I'll bet anything that what she's going through is harder. You need to be the adult in the situation and be there for her, even when it's hard."

"I know," he says. "I know."

We sit in silence next to each other for a few moments before he speaks again. "Does it ever feel like no matter what we do, we're doing the wrong thing?"

I chuckle. "Yeah. I'd say I feel like that most of the time."

"Why do we keep torturing ourselves?"

I blink, waiting for him to say more, but he never does. "What do you mean?"

"Our separation. We're trying so hard to make things work between us, but doesn't it feel wrong? We've never really worked, have we?"

I bring my hands to my temples, not believing what I'm hearing. "If you've always felt that way, why did we get married in the first place?" He opens his mouth to speak, but I cut him off before he can. "Don't try to say you loved me. I know that's a lie."

He sighs and takes a seat on the bench. "I wanted to do right by you. To do what was best for Jo."

I shake my head. "You were worried about what people would think."

"That's not–"

"Please don't try to rewrite history. You didn't do it for Jo. Or for me. You did it for you." I take a deep breath. "But I agreed. All this time I've done what you wanted. I've played the part of the dutiful wife and co-parent. I did everything you asked of me."

He hesitates, but I don't remove my stare until he finally speaks. "I'm not so sure if we did the right thing. I mean, don't you ever regret it?"

"Of course I do sometimes, but it is what it is."

"There was someone else, right?"

His question takes me by surprise. In all these years, he's never asked me that.

"I have never been unfaithful to you."

"No, I know that. I mean... before. There was someone else? Someone better? Someone... right?" By the look on his face I can tell that he already knows the answer. Maybe he's always known.

"Of course there was," I admit, at a volume so quiet that I didn't even know it was possible.

He smiles softly. "Who was he?"

"What does that matter?"

"Do you still think about him?"

I almost laugh, just out of sheer confusion that this conversation is even happening. "Sure. Sometimes."

He closes his eyes and takes a deep breath in. "I've thought about Maria every single day for the past sixteen years."

I blink. "I didn't keep you from her," I remind him. "In fact, if I'd have known, I would've told you to go back to her. The only one stopping you, was you."

"I know."

"*You* were the one who insisted we get married. I never pressured you. I said we didn't have to. I said I'd be fine, Jo would be fine, but you said we *had* to get married."

"I know!"

I look at him and my expression softens. He knows he's the only one to blame. And that blame is killing him.

"Kevin–"

"I did what I thought was right. I made my decision and I never went back." He looks down for a moment, but quickly looks back up to meet my gaze. "I'll never see her again. And that's my fault. We built a pretty good life together, but we both know we made the wrong choice."

I put my hand on his arm and quietly ask him, "What was she like?"

He smiles. It's a bittersweet smile, but it's a smile nonetheless. "She was incredible. I mean, she was the kindest person I'd ever met. She cared about everyone. Really, truly cared. And she loved to laugh. She loved to make me laugh. She just never wanted to take anything too seriously. She looked at the world and somehow managed to see through all the bad. She noticed things. Amazing little things." His voice begins to crack. "And she was beautiful. She was so, so beautiful."

"She sounds like a wonderful woman."

"She was." He shakes out his body, collecting himself. "What about him?"

I shake my head. "It doesn't matter."

"Did you love him?"

"What difference does it make?"

He shrugs. "I just want to know. Isn't it time we finally talk about this stuff?"

I guess it is time we both start telling the truth. I lean back against the wall and just listen to the thumping of the music coming from the next room for a few moments.

"Yes." I turn my head to look at Kevin. "I loved him. But that was a long time ago."

"What happened?"

I sigh, debating how much to reveal. "He had to move away and we didn't think the whole long distance thing was going to work out. We agreed that whenever he came back, if it was meant to be, it would be. And for a while I did believe that it was meant to be. But I guess it wasn't."

"You should tell him."

I laugh. "What?"

"You still love him. I can tell. Maybe he feels the same way. Maybe it *is* meant to be."

"Kev, this all happened ages ago. It's ancient history. You keep talking about how you made your choices. Well I made mine."

"But there's still time to fix your mistakes. You can change your mind." He grabs onto one of my hands and looks deep into my eyes. "Meg, it's too late for me. But for you, maybe it doesn't have to be. Maybe you can make a different choice now. The right choice."

I don't say anything.

He smiles, and it's a true smile. "I was never the one for you, but he might be. Why not give it a chance?"

I take a deep breath in and out. "Does this mean it's really over?" I ask. "Are we giving up on the trial separation and officially getting divorced?"

"Don't you think we will both be happier if we do?"

I pause for a moment to think about it, but I already know the truth. I've always known what would actually make me happy. "Yeah. We probably both will."

"Then yes," he says. "It's really over. We can tell the girls tomorrow."

We smile at each other. And everything feels lighter.

9

Ordinary World

Kevin

"Elena," I say, putting my hand on her shoulder. "Could we talk? Please?"

She turns around to face me. Her friends glare at me.

"What is there to talk about?"

"I want to apologize," I say softly. She doesn't respond, so I address the table instead. "Could I steal my daughter away for a few minutes?" A few of the kids look to Elena for guidance. Some of them just keep glaring at me.

"It's fine guys," Elena nods. "I'll be right back."

She begrudgingly follows me out of the banquet hall and into the lobby. Elena crosses her arms and avoids eye contact. God she looks so much like her mother.

"Do you want to sit?" I ask.

She shrugs, but heads over and sits down on a nearby bench, so I do as well.

"It's true," I start. "I'm not happy that you're suddenly here after years of me not even knowing about you."

She scoffs. "Great apology."

"I'm not finished," I assure her. "I'm not happy about the circumstances because frankly, they're bad circumstances."

"Are you going somewhere with this?"

"I'm overjoyed to finally know you and have you here." I choose my next words carefully. I know I have to say this just right. "But the reason you're here is awful. I loved your mother. I can't believe she's gone." I take a deep breath, almost losing track of my point.

"Every time I look at you, all I can think about is what could've been. It breaks my heart that I wasn't there for you both for the first fifteen years of your life." I notice that her eye makeup is smudged around the edges, likely from tears she cried earlier, and I hate myself because I know it was because of me. "It's hard to be your father. Not because I don't want to be, but because I don't know how to make up for all the time that I missed."

"So you decided to not even try at all?" she asks, her voice a little strained.

"I'm still figuring out how to do this."

"But there's nothing for you to figure out," she insists. "I saw all those pictures of you and Jo. You were a good dad to her. Just be one to me too."

I sigh. "You're right."

"I wish you'd been there too," she admits. "You weren't and I've made my peace with that. But you're here now. *I'm* here now."

"I know. I've been selfish. I was so caught up in my own grief, that I didn't think about how much harder this all must be for you. I should've been helping you through it, not making it worse. I can never apologize enough for what I've done and what I've said," I say, starting to tear up a little myself. "I can never make it up to you. But you're right that I haven't even been trying. And if it's not too late, I'd like to finally start." I put my hand on her shoulder again, as some sort of test, I guess, to see if she'll let me.

She looks at me, and she still doesn't smile, but she looks just a little bit less sad, and that's enough for now. "I guess it's not too late."

I let out a sigh of relief and force myself to choke back any tears that have been threatening to fall. "Well, uh..." I'm not sure if I should push my luck, but I think about what Meg said. I'm the parent. I have to go the extra mile and extend the olive branch, because it isn't Elena's responsibility to fix everything that's broken between us. It's mine. "What do you think about maybe moving back into my apartment... if that's what you want?"

She fiddles with her thumbs, and I think I've gone too far, asked for too much, too soon. But then she speaks, without looking at me, and so quietly that I can barely hear her. "I think that's a good place to start."

10

Unavoidable

Zeke

Elena doesn't notice me when I come out to the lobby, so I don't say anything at first. She looks peaceful, more so than I've seen her look in a while.

I touch her shoulder gently. She turns around and smiles at me.

"Hey," I say softly. "I just wanted to make sure you were okay."

She lets out a deep breath. "I'm okay." She often doesn't mean it when she says that, but this time I believe that it's the truth.

I smile. "Good."

I glance around, not quite sure where I should look.

"Do you want to sit?" she asks. "Unless you want to get back to the party, which you probably do, so don't worry about it, forget I asked."

She looks away from me. I can't tell if she's blushing or if it's just her makeup.

I sit down and place my hand on hers, slowly intertwining our fingers. "It's not much of a party without you anyway."

She looks down and I know exactly what she's thinking. We're supposed to be friends, but I'm not acting like a friend right now. Because I don't want to be her friend.

"You look beautiful."

She's still not looking at me, but I think I see her roll her eyes. Then she smiles gently. "Thanks."

I wonder if I shouldn't have said that. She doesn't really look like herself with her hair all done up and wearing so much makeup. She definitely didn't pick out that dress. But even under all that, she still looks amazing. She always looks amazing.

I shift a little bit closer to her even though I know I shouldn't. She doesn't move away from me. I use the hand that isn't holding hers to brush a small piece of hair out of her face. We look deep into each other's eyes and against my better judgment, I begin to lean in closer.

"Don't."

I quickly retreat, shifting away from her. "I'm sorry." I'm an idiot. What was I thinking?

"We can't keep doing this," she says. "I said that last time. We really can't, okay?"

I clasp my hands together and put my elbows on my knees. "Okay." I have to respect what she wants, no matter how badly I want something else. She's already been through so much, I don't want to be the cause of any more pain in her life.

I look at her, hoping it's not too obvious how sad I am. But before I can say anything else, she leans forward and grabs my face, pressing our lips together. At first I'm too stunned to think. Then I pull her closer and for a minute, nothing else exists.

But then my thoughts return and reality hits, so I pull away.

In a breathless gasp I whisper, "you *just* said we can't keep doing this."

She leans back and covers her face with her hands. "I know."

"Why *can't* we? Would it actually be such a problem if we were together?" I ask. "I really don't think Brooke will care."

She smirks. "Have you met Brooke?"

"Okay, you're right. She'll flip out," I admit, "but she'll get over it. Eventually."

She shakes her head. "I feel like she and I have finally gotten past everything that happened with Dylan," she explains. "If I start dating her brother, I'll mess that all up again."

I put my arm around her and she rests her head on my shoulder. "I understand. It's not your fault my sister is such a drama queen."

She jabs me lightly in the side and I chuckle softly. I can't see her face, but I can feel that she's smiling. We sit like this for a while. I'm not sure how long. It feels like forever, but at the same time, it doesn't feel nearly long enough.

11

Play Pretend

Levi

I sit back down at my table with the rest of my friends.

"That was quick," Parvati says to me. "What happened? Is she okay?"

A few minutes ago, I got up and went out to the lobby to check on Elena. I almost followed her when she first ran out during the slideshow, but her entire table got up after her and I felt like I shouldn't intrude. Then after she eventually came back inside, she left again with her father. I definitely didn't want to intrude then. But after a while, her dad came back in and she didn't, so I went out to the lobby to check on her. I didn't know she wasn't alone.

"Yeah I think she's okay," I say. "She's, uh, talking to a friend. I didn't want to interrupt."

Parvati raises her eyebrows, silently waiting for me to continue, but there's nothing else I want to say. She gives up on getting any more information out of me, for now at least. I'm sure she'll force the rest out of me later, when there's less of a crowd. She's always been good at that.

"Poor girl," says Olivia. "I can't imagine not having my mom at my sweet sixteen."

"Oh my god, your sweet sixteen was so much fun," Danielle giggles. She has definitely been sneaking real Jojitos instead of the mocktail version. I give Parvati a look. We've been friends for so long, we can communicate without words. She understands me completely and offers Danielle a glass of water and a dinner roll.

I haven't really hung out with Elena that much since everything that went down with Dylan. It feels like whenever I try to do the right thing, I end up doing something wrong. Even now, I stupidly went to check on her and she was kissing another guy. She obviously doesn't need my help at all. It was dumb of me to think she would.

I'm not jealous of course. We're just friends. Elena is great. She's smart and beautiful, but we're just friends. Nothing ever actually happened between us. I mean, she did kiss me once and I kind of wanted to let her, but I shut it down. She was in no state to be kissing anyone and I didn't want to take advantage of her when she was so vulnerable. But after that I never really got another shot.

It's probably for the best though. She's been through a hell of a year and I'm leaving for college in a few months anyway. It would be stupid to try to start anything up at this point. One of us would end up getting hurt, and the last thing I'd ever want to do is hurt her. I want her to be happy. I hope that Zack guy makes her happy. She deserves it.

Parvati seems to sense that I need a distraction, because she immediately stands up and announces to the table, matter of factly, "I think we need to dance."

12

Secrets

Jo

"Hey," I say as I take a seat next to Marisol, who is pushing food around their plate absentmindedly.

"Hey," they reply, without looking up.

"You alright?"

"Yeah."

I can tell they're lying, so I shift my chair to better face them. "No you're not. What's going on?"

They shrug. "Nothing."

"You can't lie to me on my birthday," I say, hoping they'll smile. They don't.

"It's not actually your birthday yet."

I roll my eyes overdramatically. "That's a technicality," I say. They still don't seem amused. "But it's my birthday *party* so you're not allowed to be sad without telling me why."

Marisol tugs at a loose thread on the sleeve of their black suit jacket before finally looking up at me. "It's not important."

"I'll be the judge of that," I insist. "Now talk to me."

Marisol looks away, lets out a deep sigh, and then looks back. "Why didn't you ask me to be your escort?"

I almost laugh. "What?"

"You're my girlfriend. Shouldn't it have been me up there?"

I blink repeatedly, a little surprised. "I didn't think you'd care," I say. "I didn't think you'd even want to."

"Of course I wanted to," they say. "Or at least I wanted you to want me to. This whole thing is important to you. And if it's important to you, it's important to me too. Why didn't you ask me?"

I hesitate, not sure if I should be honest, but my silence only seems to make Marisol more annoyed.

"We've barely spent any time together tonight," I continue. "Sometimes I feel like we're not on the same page. Like you don't really want me to be part of your whole world. Like maybe somewhere deep down you still want to pretend you're straight, to pretend you can still have that life."

I shake my head. "That isn't what I want." I don't even register the words until I've already said them. Wasn't I just thinking about this earlier? Wasn't I just wishing that I could have the easy life that I always thought I was supposed to want? But suddenly everything feels different. Everything seems so clear. That isn't what I want. It truly isn't. Because I want *this*. I want Marisol.

"I haven't told the rest of my family yet," I explain. "My grandparents, my aunts and uncles, none of them know about us... about me."

Marisol's entire demeanor changes. They unstiffen and any animosity fades away in an instant. "I didn't know that."

"I should have told you. I'm sorry. I didn't want you to think it had anything to do with you. It's just my dad. He said I should wait. He didn't want there to be drama at the party." My breathing shortens slightly, but this time it's not because I'm nervous. Somehow I feel calmer than I've ever felt. "But I can't blame him entirely. I didn't argue. I should have, but I didn't. I'm so sorry."

"I get it," Marisol assures me. "I mean, you think my lola[1] knows about me?" They almost laugh, but not really. "I guess I just thought it would be different for you. Easier. When you told your mom, she understood immediately. Mine is still... getting there. I didn't think you had to worry about your family. But I shouldn't have assumed that. I'm sorry."

"I didn't realize you had problems with your mom."

Marisol shrugs. "It's whatever."

---

[1] Lola is the Filipino word for grandmother.

I never really thought about how lucky I am to have my mom. I know she will love me no matter what. Even if nothing in my life ever goes as planned, she'll still always be there for me. Not everyone can be who they are, but I can. Some people may never accept me, but the only people who actually matter already do. Anyone who doesn't isn't worth worrying about. So why am I still hiding?

The deejay puts on a slow song and I know what I have to do. I stand up and extend my hand toward my incredible partner.

"Marisol Castillo, may I have this dance?"

They smile. "It's okay Jo. You don't have to do this."

"I know," I say. "I want to. It would be an honor and a privilege to dance with you tonight."

They blush and bite their lip, averting their glance. When they look back I'm still standing in the same position, looking at them in the same way, waiting for their answer.

Marisol takes my hand, and stands up, smiling just a little bit wider now. I lead them out into the middle of the dance floor, and I hold them tight as we look into each other's eyes and let the music guide us. I don't know if my family sees us because I don't care. All I care about right now is Marisol.

Younger me thought she knew exactly how her life would play out, but she was wrong. This is so much better than she could've ever imagined. I don't need a boyfriend to be happy. And I definitely don't need a so-called best friend who won't accept me. I have better friends now. And I have Marisol. And that makes me happier than ever.

Maybe my life can be alright, even if it's not the picture perfect one I thought I should have. Maybe it doesn't matter that my dress didn't fit at my sweet sixteen or that I had to share my party or that my sister ran out crying in the middle of dinner because this day was still amazing, even with the bumps along the way.

So maybe it'll also be fine that my family is changing, because sometimes what we plan isn't actually what we need. If my parents decide to stay together, it'll be great. But if they don't, I think maybe it could still be okay.

13

Stressed Out

Nico

When I see Jo and Marisol together on the dance floor, at first I think my eyes must be playing tricks on me. Didn't she tell me she couldn't come out to her entire family? If she's trying to keep it a secret, slow dancing is a pretty risky move.

But then I notice her face and realize that she knows exactly what she's doing. She's...

being herself. She's not worrying about what other people think. I feel stunned. She's not that kind of person. She is the kind of person who always cares what other people think. I know that, because I'm the same kind of person. That's one thing Jo and I have always had in common.

I was a little surprised when Jo asked me to be her escort. I figured she had asked someone else first and he said no, so I was her backup plan. We've known each other since we were infants, but we aren't really friends.

We were really close when we were younger, but some time in elementary school we learned that boys and girls couldn't be friends anymore, so that was that. I don't think either of us understood why that was the unwritten rule on the playground, but neither of us would ever go against the status quo. We just weren't like that. We cared what other people thought.

Somewhere in the back of my mind, I always kind of thought she and I might end up together. Our parents had been joking about it for years. Even as a little kid they used to call her my girlfriend. When we started high school, I even attempted to flirt with her, but she didn't seem to be interested. So I took the hint and asked out her friend Rachel instead.

I guess now we know why she wasn't interested. And now she doesn't care what other people think. I still do.

I look around the room trying to gauge the reaction from Jo's extended family as they all slowly notice what's happening on the dance floor. Some look surprised. Some seem confused. Some of them are clearly trying very hard to hide their negative thoughts. A few aren't even trying to hide them at all. Her grandmother looks downright furious. But through it all, Jo doesn't seem to care. She is completely focused on Marisol.

Maybe afterwards she'll think about the consequences of what she's done. Maybe she'll wish she hadn't done it. Maybe she'll go right back to worrying about what other people think. Or maybe she won't regret it all. Either way, right now, she's being braver than I'll ever be. She's doing something I'll never be able to do.

Part Three:
After

14

Hanging By A Moment

Meg

He's right there. He's standing by his car, checking his phone as he waits for his son to finish saying goodbye to his friends. The man I should never have let go of is *right there*.

Kevin lost the one he loved, but the man I love is standing only a few feet away from me. So why am I still standing over here?

"Harry!" I call out.

He looks up from his phone as I run toward him.

"Hi Meg."

I look into his eyes and take a deep breath. There's a lump in my throat and I can't remember the last time my heart was beating this fast, but I can't stop. I need to do this. Now.

"It's over," I say. "Kevin and me. It's over. Officially. We're done. For good."

His lip twitches as he tries his best not to smile. "Really?"

I nod. "He's never been the one for me. You should know that better than anybody."

"I should?"

"You're the one for me. It's always been you. Please tell me it's not too late."

He lets himself smile fully. "Better late than never. So... now what?"

I shrug. "Whatever we want."

I smile, and I'm sure I'm blushing, but I don't care. He scans the rest of the parking lot to see who else is around, but to me it doesn't really matter anymore. I can't wait any longer. We've already waited so long. I grab his shirt and pull him closer.

We kiss, like we should've been doing all along.

15

Last Dance

Elena

The remaining party guests have pretty much cleared out by now, meaning it's time to start packing up everything and head home. Jo and I are supposed to be helping, but instead we're picking at the leftover cupcakes. With everything that happened, I sort of missed most of dinner.

"You know what," Jo says, "I'm actually really glad we got to do this together."

"What?" I laugh as I lick a dot of bright pink frosting off of my finger. "No you're not."

"Okay, you're right, I'm not." Jo smiles. "But I had fun anyway."

"I actually did too."

"Really? You liked it?"

"Yeah, I did."

"Elena! Jo!"

We both turn around to see Ren sprinting towards us. His momentum makes him slide even after he's tried to stop. Jo and I instinctively move out of his way, but that just sends him flying into the table behind us.

"What's going on?" I ask, helping him regain his balance.

"Saw...outside...they..." He pauses in an attempt to catch his breath.

"Use your words." I tell him.

"I..." He breathes heavily.

"Spit it out," Jo snaps, impatiently.

He looks at her and takes one more deep breath. "I just saw my dad kissing your mom."

Jo blinks. She looks at me, but I have nothing helpful to offer. We both look back to

Ren for any sort of follow up information, but he's silent with wide eyes. He looks towards me, then back at Jo, all of us too stunned to say anything else. Finally Jo breaks the silence.

"What the fuck?!"

Acknowledgements

I would like to thank my family for their unwavering love and support. I also want to acknowledge my friends and my community for inspiring me and making my life richer in many ways. I especially want to thank anyone who ever invited me to their sweet sixteens, bar and bat mitzvahs, and other extravagant parties. An extra thanks goes out to those of you who served as unpaid beta readers. I also could not have finished this book if not for the love I received from my sweet dog Lily. You're a good girl.

About the Author

Ian Rose Castro (he/they) was an avid reader as a child, but as a queer Latine teen, he always wished he could see more characters like him and his friends in the books he read. He has always loved creative writing, so he decided to try writing his own.

Ian graduated from Drexel University magna cum laude, with a B.S. in Music Industry, dual minors in Communication and Business Administration, and a Certificate in Creative Writing and Publishing. He loves to listen to music, binge trashy TV, and cuddle with his dog. He currently lives on Long Island.

9 798227 130730